The Enchanted Tree and other Short Stories

The Children of James Brindley
Primary School

DEDICATION

Dedicated to all aspiring story writers - everywhere

The Enchanted Tree

CONTENTS

FOREWORD

The imagination on show in the stories in this book is testament to possibility. Children are not yet bound by convention of thought and their world makes sense. The themes that interest children are also obvious; fantastical places; characters with magic at their fingertips; families; friendship; hopes and fears.
The latest volume of stories penned by the children at James Brindley summarises all that is important to children and gives an insight into a world that we can all inhabit if we choose to.

Many thanks to Mr Kingsley for his time and his support of the children's work when collating and editing this book

C. Moore
Headteacher
James Brindley Community Primary School

The Three Little Hedgehogs

Annabelle Horton

Year 1

Once upon a time there lived three little hedgehogs. One day, they decided to make their own houses. The first hedgehog built a house out of bricks. She was very, very pleased with the house. The second hedgehog built a house of gold. He thought that it was good because it was shiny. It looked good so he was pleased. The third hedgehog was the biggest hedgehog. He built his house out of steel and it was very strong. One day the big, bad sheep said, "I'll blow and blow and blow your house down. "The big, bad sheep did the same to the golden house but the big, bad sheep could not blow the steel house down so he got angry. He also knocked his teeth out and he was never to be seen again. The end.

Three Little Kittens

Jetemi Bammeke

Year 1

Once upon a time, there were three little kittens. The first little kitten thought that fur was a good material for a house. But a big, bad dog saw the building and said, "I'll bark and I'll bark and I'll scratch your house down." Then the kitten ran to his brother's house. The second kitten thought that cotton wool would make a good material for a house. But the dog had been watching the kitten make his house and when he had finished he said, "I'll bark and I'll scratch your house down." Then the little kittens went to their eldest brother's house. He had thought that metal was the strongest material for his house. But the dog still barked, "I'll bark and I'll scratch your house down." But the dog had a shock because it wouldn't blow down and he also hurt his paw on the glass windows.

The Three Little Tadpoles

Makayla Zhang-Ng

Year 1

Once there lived three little tadpoles. They left their mother tadpole so they could make it on their own. The first tadpole made a house of lily pads. He thought that they would make a good house. The second tadpole made a house out of green, green leaves. The third little tadpole made a house of water and he thought that would make a very good house.

But then a big, green scaly crocodile came to destroy their houses. He ate the second little tadpole's house in a big, big gobble!! He ate it in one go!! And they lived happily ever after.

The Three Little Cats

Mila Grace Mawdsley

Year 1

Once upon a time, there were three cats and a big, bad fox came along. He saw a house it was made of leaves. Then he made another house. It was made of grass. Then he made another house and it was made out of trees, but a squirrel was in the tree. He was getting annoyed because he was destroying his house. So the squirrel got all the apples from the tree and threw them on the foxes head. After that the fox ran away and he never came back!

The Three Little Parrots

Thomas Evans

Year 1

Once upon a time, there lived three parrots. They left home one day to build their own houses. The littlest parrot thought that a paper house would be good. The next day, the second parrot thought a cardboard house would be good. The biggest parrot thought that a house made of cobbles would be good. One day, a chameleon came and punched the paper house down. Then he punched the cardboard house down. He tried to punch down the cobblestone house down but it didn't work. So the chameleon climbed on the roof, but he was too heavy and he fell off and hurt his back.

Laila and the Special Adventure

Gabi Judd

Year 2

Once upon a time, there was a girl called Laila. It was bed time. She dreamt of going to the park on a special adventure.

Suddenly, a huge, scary tiger jumped out and wanted to eat Laila, but brave Laila was not scared. She began to fight with the tiger. Laila was so happy that she won.

She carried on walking through the park where she met a kind fairy called Elsie.

Laila wished for her mother to come and join her dream. Elsie, the fairy, waved her wand and her mother magically appeared. Holding hands, they carried on walking through the woods.

They came to a beach and they met a group of friendly pirates who offered to sail them home.

Suddenly, Laila felt somebody was shaking her.

"Wake up Laila. It's time for breakfast." Mum called. They lived happily ever after.

Human Adventure on the African Plain

Isabelle Turner

Year 2

Walk further into the African plain, you will see some animals fighting and the lions are the Kings. The elephants are swinging their trunks around. The leopards are snoring and the buffaloes are snoring loudly. But then a human arrived and saw what was happening. The lions ran to him, but the human ran away. There was a big, huge rock and the human ran behind the rock and he saw a door. He went inside and there was a long staircase and he went down the staircase where he saw some paintings on the wall. He followed the paintings and saw pictures of humans with animals. There were skeletons all around. The skeletons were really scary and then a strange noise made him jump and he ran back out of the cave. He saw a second human looking after the lions. The first human came to him and he said, "how did you look after the lions?"

The second human said, "you just have to be nice to them!"

The first human said, "but how do you be nice to them?" The second human said, "don't run away from the lions and you won't get eaten!" The second human explained how he learned to play with the lions by stroking them and spending time with them. He also slept with the lions and played with them every day and every night until they began to like him. So the human decided to go and stay with the leopards because he was scared of the lions. After the leopards, he went to the elephants and then to the buffaloes and then to the rhinos. When he went back to the other human, and the lions, the human was thrilled to have him back. The humans stayed together with the animals for ever and ever and were never scared of any animal again.

The Two Girls and the Enchanted Tree

Isla Barton

Year 2

One sunny, summer morning there once was two little girls called Isla and Gabi. One day they went to Parr Fold Park together and they went into the woods and saw a tree with silvery, gold glitter on it. When they looked closely, they could see a door in the bark of the tree. Isla said, "this has got to be a dream." But Gabi knew the tree was magical.

Gabi walked up to the tree. She started feeling really weird and everything started to spin and the next minute she was stood next to Gabi in a magical land with pink toadstools and purple polka dots. The grass was so shiny green that it looked like it was made of emeralds. Isla and Gabi were really excited and they let out a happy scream and they also started to jump about. Nearby there were two fairies who thought they heard someone in trouble. As quick as they could, they flew to where the screaming was coming from. When they got closer, they realised it was two human girls. They quickly dived behind a rock because fairies are never allowed to let humans see them. The fairies, Alexandra and Laila, whispered to each other, "what are we going to do? Humans are not allowed in the enchanted forest! How did they get in?" They decided it was best to tell the queen and off they flew.

Meanwhile, Isla and Gabi were having a great time exploring the enchanted forest. "Hey Gabi did you just see something over by those rocks?" said Isla.
Gabi replied, "yes I did I'm sure I saw some wings maybe it was fairies. Shall we follow them?"
"Of course," Isla replied and off they ran in the same direction as Laila and Alexandra.

After some time, Alexandra had a funny feeling they were being followed so they hid in a tree and saw Gabi and Isla were following close behind. "Oh no," said Laila "we can't show them where the queen is. They will want to steal us. Humans are bad."
"Yes," said Alexandra "they are so big and mean. What are we going to do?" Alexandra and Laila started to cry. (Did you know that when a fairy cries a unicorn will always come to help within a few seconds?) Suddenly, there was a golden flash and unicorn Isobel appeared!! Isobel had a golden mane, silver wings and rainbow hooves. She was also the kindest of all of the unicorns. Laila and Alexandra were so relieved to see her. They knew that Isobel would definitely know how to help them. They quickly explained they were being followed and were scared and the humans had come to steal all the fairies. Isobel listened quietly and when they had finished she said, "oh don't worry they are nice humans. I've been watching them for a long time and we should go and say hello." Just as they were about to set off, they heard a rustle in the tree and there was Isla and Gabi. Gabi looked so shocked it was the first time she had seen a unicorn and fairy Laila said, "don't be scared. We are really friendly and we've never met humans before. How did you get here?
Isla and Gabi replied, "it's a long story but please can

you show us around a little bit?"

"Of course," said Isobel. "Climb onto my back".

First they flew to the refreshing, rainbow fountain and then they went to the fairy supermarket that was stocked with every sweet you could imagine. Isobel took them to the most amazing places. In fact there were so many that we don't have time to tell you about them all. Isla said, "this is the best day ever. Can we come and live with you?"

"Sadly we don't have a house that is big enough for you but can visit whenever you want," said Alexandra. Also Laila gave them a special gem that they could use to talk to each other whenever they wanted to. Isla and Gabi gave the fairies a big hug. "Thanks for a fantastic day. It is getting a bit late, so I guess we should head home," said Gabi. Isobel flew them to the tree with the magical door and in just a few seconds they found themselves back at Parr Fold Park. This really was a day they will never forget. What made it even better was that with their gem they could speak to their new friends whenever they wanted.

Dave the Elf

Phoebe Quayle

Year 2

Once there was an elf called Dave who was a very cheeky elf. He liked to get up to mischief, like the time when he scrunched up some of Santa`s important pieces of paper and the time he drew on Santa's precious wall with a red pen. Oh…. and then there was the time that he put slime in the toothpaste tube, so Santa had to brush his teeth with slime!!

One day, Santa was working in his workshop and writing a very important list. He needed to copy from another list, but it was gone… completely gone!! This cheeky elf hadn't realised that all this mischief was going to stop the good children getting any toys! It was the good list and naughty lists he had scrunched up!! What would Santa do? Without these lists, Christmas would be ruined! He wouldn't know which children had been good enough to get toys. Santa asked all his elves if they knew where the lists had gone, but Dave blushed and said he hadn't seen them. This made him feel bad because even though he liked being cheeky he didn't like lying and didn't want to get told off by Santa. What was he going to do? He went to Santa's workshop to find the scrunched up paper he'd hidden in the pencil pot and he put them on the table for Santa to find.

Just as Santa was about to cancel Christmas, he decided to have one last look and he found the lists! He couldn't believe it! He asked Dave if he had hidden them and Dave said nothing at first, but later on he said yes, it had been him. Santa was so pleased that he'd owned up to it that he didn't mind that Dave had lied and he still got some special Christmas presents.

The Curious Six

Dylan Zhang- Ng

Year 3

Long ago, there lived six curious children who all lived in the same neighbourhood. Every Sunday, they would have a meeting about a mysterious man who lives in a colossal farm near Pontcysyllte Aqueduct. The six children were called Billy, Max, Tim Ruby, Lily and Olivia. They all lived in a tiny quiet town called Wrexham in Wales. Tim and Olivia were brother and sister. Billy and Max were twin brothers.

The children thought the man seemed very mysterious because nobody had ever visited him. Nor had he ever talked to anyone apart from his huge, black dog named Ralph. Something even more suspicious is that on every 19th April, he would go to the canal near the aqueduct, along with his own friend Ralph. When they arrived, he would drop a bunch of different shaped and coloured leaves in the long, sparkly and peaceful canal that looked like a splendid Tadpole Galaxy.

In the middle of the Eater holiday, the Curious Six were planning a new meeting in his magnificent treehouse which he called CS Agent Hideout. On that foggy and damp Sunday morning, Billy woke up extremely early because he had to text his gang about the special password to enter CS Agent Hideout at 6:30 a.m.

It's almost time for the meeting. Obviously, Billy and Max arrived at first as the tree house was right outside their beautiful garden. Their mum had been working hard in the garden to grow all her flowers and plants. Five minutes later, Tim and his sister Olivia arrived outside of the treehouse. They whispered the password and secretly sneaked in. Later, Ruby and Lily arrived. Of course, they entered the treehouse with the tricky password. Quickly, they had the meeting and discussed their jobs. So Lily, Ruby and Olivia were going to record what the man would be doing at the Aqueduct. At the same time, the boys would sneak in the man's mysterious farmhouse and find some clues about his family.

After the meeting, they all went to the man's massive farmyard. They hid themselves behind the large haystack, so the man couldn't see them. Not long later, the man came out from his house, he looked like he didn't sleep long enough. He had scruffy, brown hair that looked like old, rotten straws. His eyes were as blue as the mysterious ocean. His old friend Ralph followed him with a miserable face. Quickly, they left the farmhouse. The three boys secretly sneaked into the man's room, and opened it gently. Then they started to looks for clues in his bedroom.

Meanwhile, the girls followed the man and his dog quietly with tip toes. At first, the man and the dog walked along the canal and picked up some leaves on the way. Then they looked like they were making some marks on the leaves. After that, they sat beside one spot that was close to the peaceful canal. Finally, he dropped these beautiful leaves into the canal and prayed with his eyes closed. He looked very guilty and depressed. Quickly, the girls took out the camera and recorded all this and ran back as fast as he could to the tree house and waited for the boys.

After a while, the boys came back with an old photo album that looked quite like an antique. Firstly, they decide to find clues from the photos. They saw a lot of photos with two young men that looked like brothers named John and Jeremy. One of them looked like the old, mysterious man, and the other could have been his younger brother. Luckily, there was a letter hiding under one of the pictures. Briefly, it said the man had been looking for his brother who accidently went missing after the boat sank on a family trip from Wales to London on 19th April 1988. The Curious Six felt heart-broken after reading the letter. Then they decided to watch what the girls had recorded. When they swathe man on the video and zoomed in. On the leaves, it said, "sorry brother, I miss you! Best wishes. John."

Al the children were shocked and their hearts were about to sink. They looked at each other and started to sulk.

William and his Dream

Sam Mullineux

Year 3

One night, William had a dream that he was a footballer. The next morning, when he went to school and told the boys in his class all about it. Their reply was "you're not gonna be a footballer!" and they laughed at him. William walked off saying to himself "I'm gonna prove them wrong"

When he got home from school that night, he told his mum what the boys had said. His mum said to him, "you ignore them...you work hard and try to achieve your dream."

These boys bullied and teased William all the way through primary school and high school, right up until Year 11, but William kept on playing football and trying his best. He ignored the boys and just when he was about to leave school Salford City called him up to play. He played for 3 seasons and scored 80 goals for them.

In his first season, they came second in League 2 and were promoted to League one. After that, they were promoted again the season after into the championship and then again the season after that into the Premiership. Then Dortmund asked if he would play for them. He scored 600 goals and won the Champions League and the Bundesliga seven times. His 600th goal was a header.

When he retired, he became manager for Manchester United then Barcelona.

The boys from school should have believed him as he proved them wrong by living his dream. It just goes to show you should never give up!

The Rainbow Savers

Max Harris

Year 3

The Rainbow was a beautiful, shiny diamond that had not been seen for 249 years. It used to be on the Earth, but a mystical, unknown creature stole it and took it back to planet Invedian. The Rainbow diamond helped everybody to become happy when they were feeling sad. Without this diamond on Earth, everyone was sad all of the time. Two astronauts called John and Jackson, travelled to space in a rocket on a mission to make the world happy again.

It took them 8 hours to arrive at Invedian and when their rocket landed, they got a shock. Outside it was 100 degrees and as wet as a rainforest. John and Jackson stepped off the rocket and began to search for the diamond with their trackers. They looked high and low... behind all of the rocks and inside caves. They could not see it anywhere, so they kept on exploring.

After hours of looking....there....on the top of a tall, rocky wall was the sparkling diamond on its own. They grabbed it, put it in the backpack and ran as fast as the wind back to the rocket. But then, Blorg appeared. Blorg is the mystical creature that stole it in the first place. He started to chase John and Jackson whilst breathing blue hot fire at them. They had to run faster and faster because the fire was catching them up. Suddenly, the diamond fell out of the backpack through a hole made by the fire. It's on the floor! Quickly, John sprinted back to the diamond and picked it up but Blorg was there waiting. He grabbed hold of John and tried to get the diamond. Out of nowhere, Jackson appeared in the rocket. "Quick John, duck!" Jackson said. He then threw out a cup of juice at the mystical creature. The juice made Blorg so sticky that he let go of John and began to squeal. John grabbed hold of the rope that Jackson had and pulled him up into the rocket. They slammed the door and zoomed away faster than a flash of light.

Eight hours later, when they got back to Earth, they placed the Rainbow diamond into an electric post to spread the happiness around the world.

The next day, when John and Jackson woke up, it felt different. They went outside and saw everyone with huge cheesy smiles and they heard lots of laughter. They were now known to the world as the Rainbow Savers. They saved the world from being sad forever. They were the best in the world!!!

Three Lions

Lucas Briody

Year 3

Once upon a time, in a place called Salford, there were three little boys called Sam, Ethan and Lucas who went to watch Salford City FC and they were very excited. The team's nickname was 'The Lions' and their favourite player was a left-back called Touray.

The weather was hot and sunny and they went with their dads and their little brothers. Sam was sat on the left side and Ethan was sat on the right side so that meant that Lucas was sat in the middle. Lucas, Sam and Ethan were all in their Bridgewater FC kits and they were still in their boots because they had played in a Bridgewater FC match earlier that day and hadn't had time to run home and switch clothes into their trainers and Salford City kits.

Before the match started, Ethan, Sam and Lucas all went to get a hotdog and the dads got chips with ketchup on top.

Then the match started and after 20 minutes they were losing 3-0. Adams had scored a hat-trick for the opponents Forest Green FC. The boys were cheering as much as they could, but it still didn't help.

At half time, 3 players from Salford City FC said they were injured and they had to stop playing and go home. Out of nowhere, the man on the speaker said, "Salford don't have enough players to play the second half. Are there any Salford City supporters here who are good at football?" The boys thought, "should we go on?" They all nodded at each other. So they did! The dads said, "You're crazy! You're only kids!"

"Yes," said the boys….we know we're kids but we are the only ones that are good at football." So they ran to the dressing room and told the manager, "We can help you out but only if you have some small kits." Luckily they did so for the second half they could play.

The second half began and the ball got kicked out of play, so Salford City got a corner. Ethan whipped the ball in whilst Sam and Lucas were in the box waiting to smash the ball. Lucas jumped up and scored a header into the bottom left corner. The dads all cheered!!!

3-1!!!

Then it was time for Forest Green to kick-off again. Off they went. Touray was surprised that three little children could actually play and score a goal. In the 59th minute, Sam ran from his own half and scored a goal.

OMG!! 3-2!!

Forest Green took a kick-off again. In the 89th minute Salford City got another corner and this time Touray took the corner so Ethan, Sam and Lucas were in the box. The ball came in high so Ethan tried something spectacular...a bicycle kick! It went into the top right corner!!

3-3!

The game carried on, but it was the 90th minute and Lucas had the ball and there were only 2 added minutes. Lucas was at the half-way line. Now he had to do something! Then an idea popped in his head...He wanted to shoot...So he did from the half-way line! It flew right into the top left corner. The match ended and Salford City won 4-3!!

The Salford City manager said, "Thank you. You can all keep your kits and come back anytime."

The dads' minds were blown and they all went home happy.

Harry Kerns

Unititled

Year 3

There was once an old, barren place that was close to forgotten, filled with all the things that no one wanted. In the middle, there was a house with big windows and in there lived a young man and a dog called Fluffles. They didn't really have many things to do. All they did was work and each day they buried, sorted and burnt the rubbish that lay in the barren place. Every night, he dreamed about diamonds and a lush valley with tropical trees and animals and flowers, birds and plants. But each new morning, it was all the same. Then one day, something caught the young man's eye and an idea planted in his head. Then one day he was going out to have his sandwich when a bird came. "Hello there and welcome! said the young man."

The bird replied, "my friend mentioned you, so I've come on my own adventure to see the forest. Is that breadcrumbs? OOO…. YUMMY!" The bird replied. He swooped down to reach the crumbs and after he had ate them he flew on a tree and perched there to sing.

But the next morning, when the man woke up, the visitor had gone. All day, he walked through the lonely, silent forest. His heart sank to the bottom of his body. But the next day he no longer felt lonely. That had all now stopped. The next day, he woke up to the sounds of birds flying in the sky. He slowly rubbed his eyes and when he looked into the air he couldn't believe what he saw. Not 1, but 2 birds were flying. One was familiar and the other looked like a friend or mate or anything like that. The birds looked like they had some seeds in their beaks and they did. The birds dropped the seeds from their beaks and then green shoots broke through the Earth. While that was happening, tropical animals, plants, trees and vines spread across the land while bugs and bees flew around the grassy plane. The roars of tigers could be heard, scaring the animals of the jungle.

There was once a wide and windswept place near nowhere and close to forgotten with all things that everybody wanted. In the middle, was a house with big windows and inside lived a dog and a man. Now they had all sorts of jungle stuff, but the only thing these two never stopped doing was dreaming. They also loved their new forest as well. They had all sorts of good adventures there and after a long day they went straight to their cosy beds.

Cross Country Time Machine

Ethan Cobley

Year 3

Chapter One

I was on the start line with forty other boys waiting for the flag to drop, but then, as I was talking to my friends, I missed the flag. Trying to catch up with other people, things weren't as bad because I was starting to climb my way to the front, running as fast as my legs could possibly carry me, fighting against the wind and rain. Suddenly, I saw a sign. Because of the wind, it had blown over, so it was not clear to see where it was telling me to go... I went left...

Chapter Two

I suddenly realised I was alone in the woods with no marshals, no runners - I knew I was lost. I ran into some bushes and before I knew it... I was somewhere I didn't know. I said to myself did I go through a time machine? No one knew. There was a code. I think I had to find the missing numbers for the code. Out of the corner of my eye, I saw something that looked very much like a number. I got closer and closer and I looked.... it was a number!! It must be for the code, so I set off looking for the rest of the numbers. I had to find six in total if I wanted to go home and to complete the race.

Chapter Three

One hour later, I finally found all six numbers. They were 6, 2, 1, 2, 5 and 1. I can finish the race!!! I thought to myself and if I come first I will get a reward from my mum! As if by magic, I appeared a short distance from the finish tunnel in tenth place. As I sprinted through the finish tunnel, I was now in second place and right before the finish line I overtook the person in first place!!! I won and I got the reward I wanted!!!

The Boy in the TV

Zac Dolan

Year 4

Finley, a blonde haired chubby boy aged nine, was walking home from school on a Friday afternoon. He was excited because the weekend lay ahead of him, which meant twenty-four hour TV watching. Finley loved to watch TV, he would wear his favourite red pyjamas. They had never been washed so they were a little bit smelly and were full of food stains!

Finley never did sporting activities, even though his parents were always trying to encourage him to take part in the local park run every weekend. But that wasn't for him, he wasn't going to get dressed on a weekend and go out in all weathers running around a silly park. He would rather sit on the sofa watching TV and eating junk food. That was the life for him! His favourite TV show was "The Cool Kidz" which was about a group of kids his age called Charlie, Emma and Tom who were famous for solving crimes. How he wished he were part of their gang. For the rest of the evening, all he did was sit on the sofa watching Cool Kidz, his mother pottering around cleaning and moaning at Finley. "You'll get square eyes staring at that screen so much," was her favourite line.

After Tea, (and another two episodes of Cool Kidz) Finley's mother told him it was time for bed. At least now his eyes would get a rest she thought! "Five more minutes mum... I've nearly finished," begged Finley. Finley's mum popped her head round the door. As she did so, she noticed that Finley seemed to be staring blankly at the TV and was not blinking. She started worrying now... She looked closely and saw the TV screen reflecting in his blue eyes. Finley's mum tapped him on the shoulder - "are you OK son?" Finley sat up startled.

"I'm fine, do I have to go to bed? It's only half eight and I've not even finished my sweets" he replied. "No arguing, Finley, it's time for bed, NOW!" Once Finley was safely tucked up in bed his mum began to worry her son was watching too much TV. First thing tomorrow she would have a word with him. If needs be.... she would take the plug off that damned TV if she had to! Finley had trouble sleeping because he was desperate to watch the next episode of Cool Kidz.

Sixty long minutes later, Finley could finally hear his parents' soft snores coming from the other bedroom. Finley didn't have a TV in his bedroom so decided to sneak back downstairs to watch another episode of Cool Kidz. First he snuck into the kitchen and grabbed some snacks quietly, and then he got snuggled up on the sofa and pressed play on the remote. As soon as he heard the music, he knew he should turn it down because it would wake his parents up. He turned it down a little to just about where he could hear it over the crunching of his crisps! Soon, he was on episode four when he began to feel sleepy. He knew he should make his way back upstairs so he would not get caught in the morning, but his eyes just wanted to close right where he lay. As he drifted off to sleep, he began to feel disoriented and he seemed to be whizzing and whirling around. Soon, he was officially lost and it felt like he was travelling in outer space - whatever that felt like.

What seemed like an hour passed but in reality it was only around twenty seconds he had been teleported from the sofa through "outer space" and into an episode of Cool Kidz.

"Hi Finley," said Emma "You're probably wondering why you are here?" Finley replied "Y…e…a…h" not being able to speak properly over his shock at seeing his heroes.

"Finley, we need your help, are you up for the challenge?" asked Charlie.

"Erm yeah," said Finley, slightly confused, "what do you need me to do?"

"We know how much you love our shows and we want you to become part of our gang and we want you to realise there is more to your evenings and weekends than watching TV in your favourite red PJs and eating junk food, (how did they know thought Finley?) We want you to become the leader of a school detective club, but first we need to know if you're the right boy for the job." Charlie, Emma and Tom took Finley on their latest crime solving adventure, which amongst other things involved a climb up the side of a small mountain. Finley soon lagged behind the Cool Kidz because he was out of breath, but he kept going even though he didn't reach the top until 40 minutes after his heroes. By the time Finley had got to the top of the mountain, the Cool Kidz had already found the clue and solved the crime without him. Finley was disappointed and felt he had let everyone down. But he was surprised to hear, "Well done Finley, you didn't give up, that's the main thing," said Charlie, Emma and Tom encouragingly. "We are proud of you. With that kind of determination you're exactly the type of person who we need as the leader of your school detective club. We have spoken to your headmaster, Mr Seymour, and he has allowed us to use your school every Friday for our club."

"WOW you're coming to our school?"

"Yep we will be there every week on one condition though."

"Anything," Finley replied, "anything, I'll do anything!"

"We want you to get together all the kids who go home on a Friday and do nothing but sit in front of the TV and eat snacks?"

"Like me?" Finley could feel the excitement inside of him and couldn't wait to get started. It was going to be the best club the school had ever had!

Suddenly, Finley began to feel the whizzing and whirling sensation again. The next moment he was back at home with his mum staring down at him and his first words were "mum, is it OK if I come on the park run with you next weekend?" Finley's mum gave a huge smile and said "Oh of course you can Finley I'd like nothing better."

The Magic Spray

Oliver Aitken-Doherty

Year 4

The main character in our story is a boy called Oliver. Oliver lived with his Mum and Dad and his little sister Sophia.

One day, Oliver was playing his favourite video game, FORTNITE. Oliver's mum came in to see what he was doing, he had been playing FORTNITE for 5 hours and his Mum wasn't very happy as he should of been tidying his room.

Oliver agreed to tidy his room, but was secretly still playing Minecraft on his tablet whilst his mum was cleaning downstairs. After 15 minutes. Oliver's mum came up to see how much tidying he had done. The answer was none! When Oliver's mum saw that he hadn't done any tidying she was now fuming and about to hit the roof! She took his computer and tablet off him until he had tidied his room, from top to bottom.

Oliver's mum went back down stairs to keep cleaning, but then she accidently sprayed the gaming controller and was instantly transported through the TV and into the world of FORTNITE. The only thing she could think to do was call for Oliver, but she had taken his games off him so he could not hear her in the game.

After 30 minutes, Oliver had finished cleaning his room and went downstairs to tell her the good news. He couldn't find her anywhere and then realised he could hear her shouting him through FORTNITE. Oliver did what all good boys would do and quickly loaded up a solo game of FORTNITE and played the game until he won and was able to get his mum out of the game.

When Oliver's mum finally came out of the TV she was pleased with how much tidying Oliver had done in his room and gave him his computer and tablet back. The next time Oliver or his mum are tidying they will make sure that the cleaning spray is not near the controllers!!

The Agents

James Evans

Year 4

Once there were two agents who worked for the company called A.A.T.W, which stands for Agents Around The World. The two agents thought it could do with a better name. The agents who were called Jim and Bob, they didn't do much, but one day Jim and Bob were sent to space on a mission for the first time. On the space ship they were told their mission, it was to deliver secret paperwork to a man in space called Mr. Plate his real name is John Plate. When they made it to planet Plate, named after Mr. Plate, the agents drank a potion which was called how to survive in space. The two agents dived out of the ship and landed just outside the castle where Mr. Plate lived. The agents ran inside the castle. As soon as they went inside the castle, there was a trap. "Already?" said Bob. The agents started to walk forward and a trap door opened as soon as possible. Bob fell down it, but Jim saved him and they carried on. When they made it to the next trap, it was a puzzle and you had to jump at the right time and if you don't another trap door will open and the agent didn't fail and they carried on. The agents made it to the next trap, this one was a laser trap, and if you touched one, another trap door would open.

The agents did it easily and ran to the next trap. The agents found out that there are three more traps, including the one they were at. So they went on to the reaction test trap and they passed it with ease. "There are only two to go," said Bob.

"Only...but we don't know how hard they are," said Jim. Later on, they made it to the next trap. It was a puzzle and you had push the right button and as you've probably guessed the agents did it as usual. The next trap was the last trap and it was a puzzle. There were a few pictures around the room and the agents had to put them in the right order! When they got to work, they did one and it was wrong, but what's the worst that can happen? Well every time they get it wrong a giant mutant animal will appear and attack you! Then a giant spider appeared out of nowhere and also attacked, but the agents had guns and shot it so that it let out a loud scream and vanished into thin air!!

Jim was so shocked at first he jumped and hid then they tried another code, but it was wrong and then a giant shark appeared and attacked. Then they shot it again and once again it let out a scream and vanished. Then they tried another but that was wrong also. Then a giant whale with armor on appeared. The agents shot it, but it took longer for it to let out a scream and vanish. Never-the-less, it happened one minute later and Bob said,"phew" and Jim was glad too. They tried another order and it was correct and then they got to Mr. Plate's office. At first he thought they were intruders and it took a long explanation, but later he understood and they gave him the paperwork. They left and then back on earth they were greeted and given the bravery award and were put in charge of the company for a day and they were always chosen to do missions, well not always of course !!

The Alien Overload

Jack Gibson

Year 4

Once upon a time, my mum and I were eating our breakfast (an English breakfast). While we were eating our breakfast, we heard on the news that there was an alien and if it touched you, you would turn into an alien yourself! The news said, 'stay away from the aliens because you don't want to be an alien.' I didn't need to worry because the aliens were in the USA (United States of America). Then, I asked my mum, can we make a trap where the aliens walk in the door and they fall into the spikes with King cobras? Mum replied, "yes okay then." After that, then we made the trap, we started to dig, dig and dig but eventually we dug a massive hole. Later on, we rang Dad so he knew that there was a trap. Once we rang Dad, we went to a place where you would find King Cobras. We got eight King Cobras in a cage. Then we went to the spike shop and got 57 spikes and then we went home. I carefully went in and put all the spikes in and then I got out of the hole. Then we put the King Cobras in and we made sure that they didn't catch the spikes. Once we had done that, I went upstairs and played FIFA 20, but sadly my team lost to Spain. Once I had finished my tournament, I went for dinner and it was a good dinner - it was pizza! Once I had my dinner, Dad came home and he had his dinner. Once he had eaten his dinner, I told him about the trap and then I went to bed. At midnight, the aliens were at our door, so I screamed at the top of my voice "Mum!!" then she woke my Dad up and we let the aliens in and they fell down the hole and died. There was a moment of silence. Then we were on the news and we got 1 million pounds and a specially made costume.

The Woodland Tree

Isabelle Evans

Year 4

Once upon a time, in a forest, there was an old oak tree. The tree had been in that very spot for years and years and it was about a million years old. Not far from the tree, there was a little house on Broom Stick Road. In the house, lived a young girl called Isabelle. Isabelle lived with her mum and her dad. Isabelle also had two best friends Mya and Lily. Mya was a very adventurous kind of girl whereas Lily liked to be organised (and disliked being dirty). As for Isabelle, well Isabelle was the kindest person you could ever wish to meet. One day, as the girls were walking to school on the Old Windmill Road, something strange happened. As they walked towards the old oak tree, they heard a faint ringing noise. "Tring...tring.....what was that?" said Lily

"I do not know," said Isabelle.

The girls put their ears to the tree and there was the ringing sound again "Tring, tring." Suddenly, a little elf popped his head out of the tree and said, "why are you knocking on my tree? This fellow is old you know!" The tree twitched, opened it's eyes and yawed. Then it said, "who is calling me old? I am young even if I do say so myself."

"Well it definitely was not me," said the elf.

"It was not you?" said the tree suspiciously. As the tree was so old and so wise, he could easily tell the elf was lying to him. The tree sighed and shook his head then muttered "he'll never learn." Then, without warning, the tree suddenly did a huge sneeze and all of its branches shot off rapidly and new ones instantly replaced them "what on earth was that!?" exclaimed Mya

"ohh that!!".... said the elf "it's just the Woodland tree's branches.. I don't know, but every time he sneezes his branches turn into broom sticks and magically fly away to good witches. Anyway, what are you all doing here?" whispered the tree.

 "Err...well....err..." spluttered Mya.

"It doesn't really matter...." said the elf. He looked the girls up and down and finally after a long pause said" Close your eyes for a minute girl..." Suddenly, there was a gust of wind and the girls found themselves sliding down a wooden slide that seemed like it would never end. At last, they slid off the slide and landed on a bouncy leaf. THUD!! went the girls as they landed. "Wow," said Lily who was the first to get back on her feet. There were lots of elves and fairies in the tree, but they all seemed sad and none of them had a smile on their faces. "What's the matter with them?" asked Isabelle. "Well…. the great gem of magic has gone. It's very precious to us elves and fairies because it keeps us protected from danger and without it we're helpless; have no magic and can't do anything."

"The witch of the East has taken it," said the elf. "She is a very bad witch and has a very large tribe of goblins." There's only one way to get it back and that's to have a magical locket that I gave to a young girl who came to this tree before you a long time ago. She's probably forgotten all about the magic fairies and stuff so that way is hopeless."

"Or maybe not," said Isabelle. She was wearing a locket and she asked, "does that locket have a love heart in the middle? And is it made of gold?"

"Yes! Yes! a million times yes!!" exclaimed the elf. Of course, that girl must have been my mum. Isabelle showed the elf the locket she was wearing around her neck. "Yes …yes… of course it is. How could I have forgotten? I gave it to your mother as a gift a long time ago. How silly of me!" And with that, the elf bounded away and came back a few seconds later with what looked like an aero plane. It was made from wood and had two leaf wings and had a steering wheel made from an acorn top. "Hop in girls!!" cried the elf "and "off we go to the land of the witch of the east."

"Let's Go!!" said Isabelle. A little while later, the elf suddenly slammed on the brakes and said "wait, wait, wait!!! I forgot to tell you my name! My name is Olly, Olly Dawn, but just call me Olly and I'm a gem keeper. Gem keepers look after these magical precious gems and it's all because of us gem keepers that this gem is lost. Because I am the leader of the gem keeps it's my responsibility to get it back".

"Well you're lucky you found us because we never run away from a challenge," said Isabelle.

"Yeah!" said Mya "we stick together no matter what happens we're friends," said Lily.

"Aahh.....thanks guys" said Olly. Whilst all this was going on, the plane dipped lower and lower in the sky and Olly spun around and his eyes widened. "Hang on we are going to have a bumpy landing?!!" shouted Olly. Bump, crash, bang! "Is everyone ok?" asked Olly.

"I think so," Lily replied. The girls all pulled themselves clear of the aero plane. "Wow. There are so many Witches hats here" observed Lily.

"What's that?" asked Isabelle, pointing to a tall Grey

eerie looking building in the distance.

"That…" continued Olly "….is the Witches Palace, and the Gem should be in there. Come on girls….." "WHO dares walk the paths of Witch Land?" came the shout from the silvery grey trees up above them. Looking up, the girls saw a small slimy looking creature, with purple horns and yellow stained teeth. "Goblins…RUN!!" called Olly, and with that they turned and fled.

"Over there!" panted Mya, pointing to a high wall "let's get behind it." After a few minutes silence, Mya was the first to whisper "phew, they've passed…now let's get on and find that gem." In a short space of time, they reached the twisted iron gates of the Palace and snuck inside.

"There are so many corridors…how we know which one will take us to the Gem?" said Mya.

"It could be that one…or that one…" muttered Olly.

"Well…I always say follow your nose so it's this way," said Isabelle. Pushing straight on, they reached the end of the corridor to an open door and went inside. "Brrr…. it's cold in here" shivered Mya.

"….and why are there so many mirrors?" asked Lily

"I have absolutely no idea," said Olly and then they heard a crunching noise and then…BOOM! – Mya suddenly became trapped within one of the large rectangular mirrors. "Help! I can't get out!!" she screamed and then there was another bang and Lily appeared in the opposite and it happened again...BOOM! – Olly came into the mirror next to Mya. "Why am I not in a mirror?" said Isabelle. "Because you have the necklace of everlasting life," said Olly "More importantly how can I get you out?" said Isabelle.... I don't know!! yelled Olly....but you must carry on without us...you must get to the Gem. Isabelle pushed on, feeling alone and scared, but kept moving down corridor after corridor until she could hear a lady's voice shouting "Where is that Gem?"

"We don't know madam," came a meek reply

"Well. Go find it!! I am the Queen of Witches so get a move on!!!" Isabelle peered around the corridor to see a group of five goblins shuffling away. Isabelle quietly followed the pack of Goblins down a set of stone steps into a cold cave, with strange sets of etchings on the wall. The Goblins tapped on the wall three times and whispered something that Isabelle could not quite hear. The wall creaked open and the Goblins snuck inside. Isabelle tried to follow, but the wall closed before she could reach it. She decided to follow suit, knocked on the wall three times but nothing happened. "What on earth is that password the Goblins were muttering?" she wondered. Right in front of her nose, a couple of bats flew by, brushing their wings against the cave walls, revealing hidden text. "Well...I never...my favourite!" thought Isabelle. She hurriedly knocked on the cave three times and gently spoke, "Cheesy Pasta!" The wall creaked open and Isabelle hurried inside. She ran down the steps to catch up with the Goblins, going faster and faster until she suddenly stopped…and turned her shoulder. Something had caught her eye, a sparkle buried into the wall. She took a closer look and brushed away the surface dirt. The sparkle became bigger and bigger. It was a gem! It was now the size of her hand, and she could make out a few small letters written onto the gemstone. "C I G A M..?" Isabelle wondered… "MAGIC!" she exclaimed, but perhaps a little too loudly. A spy shouted to the Goblins "There she is! "pointing their bony fingers towards Isabelle "and she has the rainbow Gem!!". The Goblins started to run towards her. As quick as a flash, Isabelle prised the Gemstone out of the wall and headed up the stairs as quickly as she could. "Cheesy pasta," she yelled and rushed out of the cave, the walls closing just in time to stop the Goblins getting past.

Back along the maze of corridors she went, but which one was the corridors back to her friend and Olly. Was it left, or right? Isabelle couldn't remember. "Left" she thought. But that was a big mistake, running straight into the Queen of Witches. "Give me that Gem, child!" the Witch screamed.

"No way!" yelled Isabelle, turning to head back. She stopped in her tracks as the Goblins had finally caught up and were now heading towards her. She was trapped.

"You're all alone child. With no-one to help you!" cackled the witch. Suddenly, Isabelle's locket began to glow. "What's going on?" yelled the witch, as all her mirrors began to suck her and her goblins towards the mirrored surface. "No…. No…you will pay for this!!!…. I will get you!!!" shouted the witch. Isabelle heard another BANG and she ran down the corridor as fast as her legs would go towards her trapped friends. Mya, Lilly and Olly had fallen out of the mirrors and were lying on top of each other in a pile on the floor. "Are you all okay?" asked Isabelle.

"We think so" said Olly, "but let's get away from here."

"Erm, one question" spoke Lily "how do we get out of here? There still could be goblins out there looking for us, the doors to the castle are locked and our plane is broken".

"Good point" said Mya. "Well, there has to be a back door or something, "said Isabelle quickly. The friends and Olly headed down what felt like the only corridor they'd not been down. At the end of the corridor was a spiral stone staircase. Isabelle put one foot onto the first step." Woah," said Isabelle as the step disappeared. The next moment, she found herself whizzing down a slide made from Gummy bears. "Where are you Isabelle?!!" shouted Olly, not knowing where she had gone. "I think she's gone down here," said Mya, pointing to the staircase. The girls and Olly followed and found themselves too whizzing down the same slide, spiraling down and down for what felt like ages. The end of the slide came into view…. and whoosh…. off they flew landing on a floor made from Marshmallows. "Mmmmm…." said Olly, picking up handfuls of the fluffy treat and putting it to his mouth.

"Olly!!!! Don't eat the floor," said Mya.

"Sorry!" said Olly in a disappointed voice. "But….I didn't have lunch". No sooner had the friends re-grouped and tried to work out where they were, when the ground began to shake.

"Hello!" boomed a voice from above them. "Who are yyyy, you??" said Lilly quivering with fear.

"I'm a jelly baby and welcome to the land of Sugar….my name is Bertie."

"This is the land of Sugar?" asked Olly, "Even I didn't know such a place existed".

"Where are you from anyway," asked Bertie.

"We're from the Woodland Tree," said Olly.

"Never heard of it," replied Bertie. "But no matter, I do know someone who could help you".

"Who?" asked everyone at the same time.

"The great master of Sugar," replied Bertie.

"Come on you have to meet him" and with that, Bertie

picked them all up and bounced across the land towards the Master of Sugar's palace. The palace came into view on the horizon, and the girls were amazed. The palace had giant chocolate gates with marshmallow roof tops, and gummy bear soldiers guarding the front. Bertie called to the guards, "I'm here to see the Master of Sugar".

"Fine" yelled the Gummy bears. The big chocolate gates opened and led them down a wide corridor with statues of past Jelly baby queens and Kings either side of them. At the end of the corridor, stood a beautiful gleaming shining throne, and sitting in it was a large creature, that appeared to be made from sugar cubes. The cubed creature boomed, "if you have something to say, then say it now. I still have to get me beauty sleep!...your highness," said Bertie. "All I would like is for you to take my newest friends, Olly, Lily, Mya and Isabelle home to the Woodland Tree".

"Hmm," pondered the cubed King.

"No way I am not wasting my magic on that plus I am having my beauty sleep now so goodnight."

"But sir..." protested Bertie.

"No buts" replied the cubed King.

"Great. Now how can we get home," wailed Lily. Olly thought for a moment "The Gem...the gem!!! We can use the Gem" shouted Olly. Bertie looked at him puzzled. "I'll explain later" said Olly, as he held the Gem high up above his head. The Gem started to glow, and the winds started to bluster. The girls were swept off their feet, spinning around and around and around. When the winds died down, they opened their eyes and realised they were no longer in the land of sweets...they had made it back to the woodland tree. Olly placed the gemstone back into a nook into the tree trunk. All the elves and fairies were happy. "Thanks again," said Olly as he led them out of the tree. "We know you trapped the Witch into the mirrors of Spirit World, but she is very powerful and may find her way out eventually. We may need your help again." The girls turned to each other and grinned "Well, we faced a lot of challenges and don't fully understand the power of this locket just yet, but if you need us, call us," said Isabelle. "Goodbye Olly" said Lily.

"Goodbye girls," Olly replied with a smile. The girls walked home slowly together.

Mya said, "what an adventure!!!! Best day ever!!....until the next time at least."

Guardians of the Chest

George Condron

Year 3

It was a snowy, winter's day and Adam and George, two normal boys, who have a normal life couldn't believe that last night, whilst they were playing football, they found a hole in the fence. They anxiously walked through it and found a magnificent looking castle (but you would know that if you have read my previous story The Guardians of the Chest)

"Rise and shine sleepy heads," said my mum.

"Ding doing" went the door

"Will someone get the door" said my mum.

Adam casually walked over to the door and opened it with an element of surprise.

 "Hey George" said Adam.

"Yes" I said.

"You might want to see this," said Adam.

There in the door stood Phil (the dragon) he was a scaly, funny and kind dragon. Adam and George were surprised to see Phil standing in the doorway. It was odd enough that a dragon would live through a hole at the bottom of your garden, but a dragon knocking on your front door was just weird.

"srtgtdfjmhfh, egrgffnyg," said Phil.

Which in dragon talk means, "the Princess needs you and will you come?" Strangely, Adam and George could understand dragon language, they must have learnt it last night on their adventure.

Adam and George looked at each other and said, "mum we're going out, see you at ten"

Then they got on to Phil and flew to the castle. On the way Phil said, "the evil king Olivier is trying to take the Princesses castle".

Phil said, "the king is really mean and likes playing with Viking toys and his best friend is a wolf and he has a pet bull shark"

Oliver is a mean, disgraceful king who wants to take over the land. Phil landed in the middle of the forest. Then George saw a shining shimmering chest. George and Adam walked over to the chest and Adam opened the chest with excitement wondering what the chest would give them this time.

Inside the chest lay the boys' ninja suits and two swords. "We've got to stop the king," said they boys as they ran towards the gold and blood red castle.

When they got to the castle, they saw a red, green and yellow door. George took out his sword and sliced the door off its hinges.

Behind the door were two heavily armed guards with name tags saying Reilly and Leo. They were both tough muscly boys. Adam distracted the guards with one of his silly jokes (again).

"Why did the chewing gum cross the road?" said Adam "because it was stuck to a car tyre," the guards laughed so hard they fell into a deep sleep. Then Adam and George silently tiptoed across the floor, ran up the stairs and came face-to-face with the king himself.

George and Adam were scared because they thought the king was mean and evil. Then, suddenly, the king started crying.

So, Adam and George asked him what was wrong. The king explained that he was just lonely. Adam and George felt sad that the king was lonely, so they had an idea. They told the king that he could be their friend.

And they all lived happily ever after………. Until part three.

GAME OVER

Thomas Wilson

Year 5

This story begins on the High Street of the happy, happy place, Shine Ville, where a 12 year old boy, Carter, was walking out of the videogame store. He had just used 4 weeks' pocket money. In his hand, a shiny blue videogame case with letters in huge font, that spelt 'The Quest of two Worlds.' It was a brand new game that Carter had wanted for months. He put the game in his bag, hopped onto his black sports bike and rode home on it. About 5 minutes later, he jumped off his bike. Before him was a small bungalow (his house). He pushed open the detailed red door and sat down on the sofa in his living room.

"Mum!!" He yelled...no answer... "Must still be at work," he muttered. He pushed the new game disk into his PS4 and then he picked up his phone and called his friend Darren. Soon Darren was at the house and had an identical controller in his hand to Carter's. They booted up the PlayStation and started the game. When they pressed start on the game menu, nothing happened. Carter clicked again and then a blinding cyan light flashed before their eyes. Carter screamed and Darren yelled, but there was nothing they could do. Then they woke up "huh!" Carter said, "what?" Darren blurted. They looked around and the house had gone, they were now in a dense rainforest, Darren climbed a tree.

Carter ducked in a hole, with the same terrified look on their faces it was clear that they wanted to go home. A hologram appeared "greetings" it said, "my name is Jeff and I will be your guide". Carter and Darren bombarded the hologramic face with questions. Jeff said that they were in the game that they had been sucked into it. They were terrified and bewildered. Then Jeff said, "now please wait where you are for a supply drop". Soon enough, two boxes on parachutes came down. The boxes contained a can of beans, an armoured vest and a HAT! Happy with their new items, the two boys set off on their quest. "Jeff," said Darren. "This game is called Quest of the Two Worlds, soooo isn't there 2 worlds."

"Affirmative," Jeff droned.

"What planet is this then?" Asked Darren.

"This world is Takadiko - a dense rainforest planet," replied Jeff. "More info on this world, it is full of tribal villages and markets and it has a dangerous animal called leafoioz. It will be your boss level opponent on this World. It lives on the minus 40'000 degree rings of the planet. You will need hyperspace suits, found in legendary crates, only found in the abandoned rocket base. It is the first and easiest boss and will be defeated easily. It is made from rock, hard wood, and palm fronds. Caution bosses are dangerous." Sirens flashed around Jeff's head. "Greifers near," he warned, and then he repeated it. "Greifers near," he droned.

Then huge spiders fell from the sky, screaming. They ran and ran until they found a huge metal building that had a huge hole in the middle, and a hole in the roof. Above the huge hole, in the middle around the build was a tall metal fence topped with barbed wire. Carter jumped the fence, Darren slid through a hole at the bottom of the fence and Darren spotted a futuristic looking gun. Jeff then droned, "hot shot added to inventory." Then Carter picked up a white stick with a button on the bottom. He clicked it and a red laser popped out of the top. Jeff then said, "lazerpro added to inventory." They ran inside the building and they realised this was the abandoned rocket base. Jeff stated, "get a hyperspace suit and find a suitable ship." They ran to get them. Hypersace suits were black and orange spacesuits with huge black visors from neck to forehead. Information was written on the inside of the visors. The boys pulled on the suits and found a ship. Jeff said it was called a T Wing X class 5.36. They hopped into the rusted old vine covered ship. Darren started it up and to his surprise lights flickered. The Ship's computer set course to 3rd ring of Takadiko. A couple of hours later, they arrived and saw the boss. Screaming, they ran, but the boss always caught up with them. Luckily, they had weapons. Darren pulled out his hot shot and shot the boss. The lazerfied pellets hit hard and pierced through his bark like skin.

Carter sliced and diced cutting the bosses arms off. Then they both aimed for it's head. Before they knew it, blinding green light flashed before their eyes and they were in a wasteland with volcanoes everywhere.

"We defeated the boss," they both screamed. Jeff appeared "Magmoz new location," he droned.

"Yay!!!!!!" they yelled "we did it, one down one to go."

The green was gone, and replaced with orange sand and black rock. They were cheering hard and loud when Carter spotted a rusted up container with a ship next to it. The ship was white and had marks where the paint had scratched off. It was small, but had rusted guns on it. They were attached to the wings and they were strapped on with duct tape. Then a figure came out of the container, his body was mangled and he wore a ripped classic spacesuit like the ones astronauts wore when going to the moon in 1969. On his head, was a cap embroidered with the words "Nebula 4 Life" on it. One of his arms was robotic. He was scary but looked….. human. Then he spoke in a low voice "what are you kids doing here?" he asked. They explained, and the man said, "ok, come in, I'll tell you about this place."

The containers interior was rusted, but, cosy. There was a fire in the centre, a bucket in the corner. At the side and around the fire there were armchairs, all in different patterns and all with springs sticking out of them. The man sat on a checked one with springs coming out of the middle and the armrests. It's cushion was also missing.

"Ok, I shall begin," the man said.

"This place is called Magmoz. As you probably already know, each planet has a boss. This planet's boss is called Inferngolem. You will find it in the great volcano. It is about 20 miles away from here, take my ship if you like?"

Carter and Darren thanked the old man and took the keys to the ship. They went outside and hopped in.

The ship had two seats, one for the pilot and one which

controlled the guns.

The old man came running out of the container. "Take these," he shouted, passing them two white featureless spacesuits. "These will protect you when you swim in the lava."

Darren took the pilot's seat and Carter manned the guns. Darren started the ship and activated auto-drive. Fifteen minutes later, they arrived at a huge volcano. They both left the ship and Darren tied the ship to a nearby fence post to avoid it being swept away in the strong wind that had started. Scared they jumped into the lava. The visor on the suit was clear, but made it possible to see

In the lava, they swam to the bottom of the pool. Then they saw the boss "ahhhhhh!!" they screamed. A huge fist made from rock thrashed through the red lava towards them. Darren pulled the hot shot out and started firing rapidly. Carter pulled out his lazerpro and cut, but the hard rock of the boss would not break.

Bullets nor blades, nothing could break him, but his head was not armoured like his body. They aimed, and fired, red light filled their view and then they were back in Carters living room.

Just then, Carter's mother walked in "have you boys had a good time? Probably saving the universe from evil bosses I bet" laughing she went to the kitchen. "Yes we did" said the boys, winking a knowing wink each other.

The Night Pilots

Yvie Cooper

Year 5

Now I know what you're thinking ...how can such an ordinary teddy bear (Freddy Teddy mind you), become a super important pilot? Well fear not fair reader. For I, Freddy Teddy, shall tell you.

It was Christmas Eve and Ethan (the boy who bought me), was in bed looking at the stars holding me in those

… things, what are they called again? Oh yeah hands …anyway then his Mum came in and said "bedtime Ethan" in her usual way and Ethan responded with an "Ok Mummy!" in his cheerful manner. Now Ethan is a boy with sandy hair and chocolate eyes who loves football, dinosaurs and me. He gently put me on the pillow next to him and turned over to go to sleep. "Night, night Freddy," he said. Then, as soon as his eyes shut, I leapt up to the window beside the bed where Ethan lay dreaming about the Cup Final or something.

I now stared out of the open window, gaping at the whiteness of the moon when I saw a red light. It hovered and then came shooting right for me. As it came closer, I could see there was something in it; a bear in fact. I was astonished, I'd never seen another live teddy bear before. The light landed outside Ethan's window on the windowsill. I now saw before me an aero plane painted red with "Ted Force One" written along it's side in white. The bear stepped lightly out of her open cockpit and said "My name is Ellie Cuddles. Nice to meet you, oh Hero of the Sky."

"Hero of the what?" I said confused.

"You're our only hope of stopping Dastardly Eric! You know; Elf, 30cm tall, him! Put on the naughty list then sacked by Santa, he's all over the news" said Ellie.

"Oh right yes, I've heard of him, isn't he the one that wants to steal toys? What did he say, 'if I can't have

Christmas, then no-one can!'?" I said in reply. "But how can I help?"

"Captain Buttons will explain everything when we get to Tedquarters. Now hop in Freddy T" she said holding out her paw.

I took it and said "How do you know my name?"

"Lucky guess," replied Ellie as she helped me in, then off we flew.

Over all the houses we flew not saying a word until Ellie said, "Hold on tight! We're goin' in!" At this point, we were over the River Thames. Ellie pressed a button, a roof came up to cover the cockpit and we went down, down underwater until we reached the opening of a cave, as black as a black hole! Ellie turned Ted Force One towards the cave and we went in.

Ellie landed the aero plane on a landing pad inside a huge, blue dome and said cheerfully, "Welcome to Night Pilots' Headquarters – Tedquarters for short". Suddenly, a bear in a tuxedo and monocle ran up to us panting and said, "Hello there you two, I'm Captain Buttons, Chief here at Tedquarters". Then he led us to a room full of screens, each with a bear sat in front of it working busily. He coughed loudly and then said, "Ladies and Gentlebears, the Bear of Hope is here!" The room fell silent and a hundred sets of eyes turned in my direction and stayed there. Captain Buttons began to speak, "Welcome to Tedquarters Freddy" he said, "I know you believed that you were the only live teddy bear in the world. You may not have heard of us before, Freddy, but we have known about you for a very long time. You are a very special bear – the kind of bear that only comes to life once a century. Your talents make you unique and we have brought you here because tonight we need your help."

I was speechless. After a few moments, I said "what talents?"

"You have the best speed and reactions of any bear alive today," said Ellie. "We need you to pilot a special aero plane tonight to help us stop Dastardly Eric's dastardly scheme to steal all of the toys Santa will deliver tonight to all the children in England! Will you help us?"

"Yes" I said. Every bear in the room cheered loudly. "Great" said Ellie, "we've no time to lose – follow me!"

Ellie now led me back to the blue dome where another bear was working on a small blue, very sleek aero plane. "Hello, I'm Ella Ted, Freddy T. This is your new plane – hop in" said Ella "Toy 2000 it's called – made it just for you".

"How do I fly it?" I asked.

"Easy" said Ella, "all you need to do is think about where you want to go, but you'll have to think quickly – this is the fastest plane we have. That's why we need you".

Suddenly, more bears wearing flying goggles rushed into the dome, jumped into the other aero planes, then took off and dived one-by-one into the tunnel that led back to the river. "Come on Freddy T, time to fly!" said Ellie jumping into Ted Force One with Ella and then taking off to follow the others.

I climbed in to the cockpit of Toy 2000, closed the cockpit roof and took flight. The plane dived into the tunnel and then a moment later I had shot from the river into the air. I found flying very easy and before I knew it I was soaring over London, using Ellie as my guide. All the other bears were up ahead, and soon I found myself in formation with everyone.

Suddenly, I heard Ellie over the radio. "Look, I can see Dastardly Eric over Buckingham Palace." I looked to my right and saw a fat, brown reindeer with one antler flying over the palace, with an elf sat on top holding a huge faded red sack bulging with toys.

"Get in formation everybody," cried Ellie on the radio, "now, after that elf!" The bears sped towards dastardly Eric and so did I. Faster and faster they flew but it was easy for me to keep up in Toy 2000.

Dastardly Eric on his one-antlered reindeer. Devious Bob saw us approaching and started to try to get away. He flew in crazy patterns through the sky as fast as his reindeer could go (which wasn't actually very fast). We bears flew up, down, left and right to surround him in the sky, but he wouldn't give in.

I flew faster than any bear has ever gone before and started looping around him and Devious Bob. Soon I was moving so quickly that I'd created a whirlwind around Dastardly Eric, who got so dizzy that he crash landed in St James' Park.

I landed and jumped out of Toy 2000, Ellie landed alongside me and we ran over to the wreckage of Dastardly Eric and Devious Bob.

Dastardly Eric lay on the floor rubbing his head. "Bah! Annoying bears!" he said angrily "I'll get you, I will … I will!" and he threw the sack of presents at me and ran off. After that, we all spent the night returning toys to the children they belonged to.

As for me, well I had many a night just like this one with Ellie, Ella and Captain Buttons, but I always came home to snuggle beside Ethan.

The Worst Day of my Life!

Ruby Pritchard

Year 5

It was just a normal school day for Ruby, but little did she know her day was about to change. She walked calmly to school with her best friends Lily, Layla, Sophia and Eliza. When they got to school, she went into her classroom and found a big, bad girl on a chair at the front of the classroom. Miss Wilding introduced the girl apparently her name was Michelle, but people called her Menacing Michelle because she was a bully. Miss

Wilding sat Michelle next to Ruby. Ruby was so scared she would hurt her, but luckily as soon as she sat down the bell went for break time.

Ruby and her friends talked about their first impressions of Michelle. Eliza said her first impression of Michelle was that she looked mean and angry, but little did she know Michelle was standing right behind her.

"What did you say about me?" shouted Michelle.

"NNNNothing," Eliza trembled.

Luckily, the whistle went for the end of break time. Ruby was even more scared now. She tried to slide away from her. For Ruby, the English lesson was a lifetime long.

The next day, Ruby didn't want to go to school because of menacing Michelle, but somehow her mum persuaded her to go. When Ruby got to school, she discovered that today Michelle bullied Lily and then the next day she bullied Layla. Suddenly, Ruby realized she was bulling her friend group, which wasn't very good because Ruby was the only one left in her friendship group.

The next day, it was Ruby's turn to get bullied. That evening, Ruby's diary read:

Dear diary,

My day hasn't been the best, but I got through it. Today I got bullied by Menacing Michelle.

It was just a normal day at school, but sadly I bumped into Michelle trying to get my toast and milk and go outside. I was talking to Sophia about what we could do at my house when she comes around. Sadly, Michelle was standing right behind me, so I had no time to run and hide. She walked up to me and said, "would you like a punch or a kick?"

"Neither," I said.

"You don't know do you? "said Michelle.

"No, I don't. "Ruby cried.

"Then you get double of both," shouted Michelle.

Everyone ran away except from Lily, Layla, Eliza and Sofia. I held my tears back as I scrunched myself up into a ball. Michelle was about to punch me… Then my friends stood in front of me and told Michelle she was a bully. She didn't take it the right way because instead of apologising she raised her foot menacingly ready to unleash the first kick. My friends ran to Miss Wilding and told her everything. She was astonished. Miss Wilding ran over to the incident quickly.

"Ruby are you ok?" asked Miss Wilding.

"Yes I'm fine." I cried.

"As for you then Michelle it's the head teacher's office," said Miss Wilding.

Michelle walked into Mr. Moore's office and hated being sent there so she said sorry to me and my friends. So, we are all friends after all.

AUTHOR'S NOTE:

NEVER BULLY BECAUSE IT COULD HAPPEN TO YOU SOME DAY!

The Magical Dog House.

Jasmine West

Year 5

In the summer holiday, a girl called Lucy was packing her suitcase to go to Spain on an adventure. Before she went, she had to take her rabbit named Sven and her puppy named Prince to the pet hotel. Little did she

71

know that it was the start of their adventure and not hers. She dropped them off, gave them a hug and drove off to start her holiday.

The next morning, Sven and Prince woke up and had breakfast together. After that, they went on a stroll through the fields. It started raining really badly, so they ran into a dog house and went inside. Suddenly, the dog house started glowing and in a blink of an eye they were transported into the world of Beatrix Potter in the Lake District!

When they got there, they started to explore. Obviously Sven was the most excited as he looked just like Peter Rabbit. They looked in their booklet of clues and activities and found Jemima Puddle Duck in the first room trying to hide her eggs from the farmer's wife.

They stopped for tea with Mrs Tiggy Winkle which was delicious then made their way to the garden where Peter Rabbit and his brothers and sisters roamed and got up to mischief.

As they were playing, the doghouse started to glow so they jumped in and it took them home.

The next day, they ate breakfast as usual and went back across the field to the doghouse. They charged in and just like that they were transported to Siam Waterpark in Tenerife.

As they walked through the gates in their swimming

costumes and goggles, they were amazed by all the slides and colours they could see. Whooooosshhhhh!!!..... They went down the 1st slide, then the 2nd and 3rd. Prince needed to stop for a break as he started to feel sick, so they went to relax at the wave pool and beach. They floated for a while in the water when they realised they were on their way back to the doghouse. They jumped in as they were both very tired and made their way back home talking about what an amazing time they had.

They both decided that they would start planning their trips in the future, so they had their tea and a much needed early night.

Dying Earth

Holly Humphries

Year 5

PROLOUGE

A million years ago our world was a happy place.

Everybody breathed in clean sweet air. There were no cars to pollute the earth or planes to put CO_2 into the air. The world was a happy place and people lived in peace. Now, most people believed that the first people on earth were Adam and Eve. They lived a happy and simple life on a lovely earth. But today our world is dying. It's like our planet is a balloon that is floating further away from us.

THE LEES

"I will finish off here," said Mrs Lee as she tidied up some papers into a neat pile.

"Ok me and Lucy will wait in the car," said Professor Lee. Now Mr and Mrs Lee both worked at NASA and they had an 11 year old daughter called Lucy. Mr and Mrs Lee and a group of other scientists were trying to find whether or not there is a planet that is capable of sustaining life. Mrs Lee had once said to Lucy that her job was very important because of what we are doing to our planet. As Mr Lee opened the big heavy doors to the car park, he said, "I'm sure we will find something soon." Mrs Lee smiled and sighed. Meanwhile Lucy was patiently sat in the car. She was flicking through the channels to see if there was anything worth listening to but it was past 10 o'clock. She sighed and slumped down into the leather seats of the car. She looked down and remembered that she had brought her phone. Lucy picked up her phone and face-timed her best friends Katy and Grace.

Grace and Katy's parents both work at NASA and that's how Lucy, Katy and Grace all knew each other. Katy had long blonde hair and dazzling blue eyes while Grace, on the other hand, had long brown hair that was always in a bun while her eyes were the colour of chestnuts. The three girls hung out all the time, but Grace and Katy didn't have to wait in the car because they could go to their Grandparent's house but Lucy couldn't. That was because her Grandparents owned a small pub on the edge of town which children under the age of 18 could not go inside.

"We didn't make the rules," Lucy's grandma said when Lucy moaned about not being able to go inside the pub. But in all fairness she did make the rules. The pub was called The Armchair and it was on the edge of Warwick Street. Lucy didn't think The Armchair was a very creative name but it didn't stop people from coming and enjoying their Friday night. As Lucy's phone rang, her dad opened the car door.

"Finally," said Lucy.
"Sorry, your Mum and I were looking at the new planet we found," said Mr Lee.
"So what did you find asked Lucy?"
"Nothing!"

"Seriously!" said Lucy, "where's Mum?"

"Still working, " said Mr Lee.

Annoyed, Lucy sank back in her seat and pressed her

ear to her phone. It rang for a minute and then went silent." Err…….. Hello " said a quiet voice on the end of Lucy's phone.

"Oh hi, " said Lucy " I defo did know that this was a Face time and not a call, " Lucy said to Grace.

"I heard that too!" said Katy.

"Where did you come from?" said Lucy.

"Grace called and said you needed us so I popped over," replied Katy.
"So anyway….. I was thinking why don't we go on a secret mission!" said Lucy sounding very excited.

"A secret mission," said Grace raising one eye brow.
"Anyway, what do you suggest we do for this secret mission?" asked Katy.
"Well let's talk about it at my place. Three, tomorrow," said Lucy.
"Why such the rush?" asked Grace.
"It's private SO DON'T TELL ANYONE!" yelled Lucy.
"Oooooohhhhhhhh…………………………. GOT IT!" replied Grace and winked.
They both shut off their phones and Lucy patiently waited for her parents.

Meanwhile, inside the lab, Mrs Lee was just packing up her stuff when she glanced at the clock on the wall. It was nearly midnight. She had been in the lab for over 2 hours! She quickly tidied up her papers and picked up her black briefcase and walked to the doors. Then she switched off the lights and opened the big heavy doors to the dark, desolate car park. She walked across the car park towards her lonely red car.

She opened the car door with a CLUNK. "Sorry, " said Mrs Lee sounding like she had swallowed a wasp.
"I was studying the new planet your Dad and I discovered," said Mrs Lee.
"And what did you find?" asked Lucy not really bothered.
"Well ………………… nothing!" replied Mrs Lee.
"So I've been waiting in the car for 3 HOURS for you and Dad to find NOTHING!" yelled Lucy
"Tough! " she said as she started the small red car. " Let's go home and gets some rest," said Mrs Lee with a yawn. But Lucy was already fast asleep as Mrs Lee drove out of the car park and down a little side street and turned into a little driveway with a small, wonky house on the edge of town.

It was the next day and Lucy, Grace and Katy were all upstairs in Lucy's bright pink bedroom. She had called her friends for a special meeting.

"So," Lucy said, "Do you guys want to find out what goes on inside the lab? "

"Well not really," said Katy looking out of the window at Lucy's next door neighbour's cat.

"Come on, it'll be fun seeing the different experiments

our parents do,'' said Lucy.

"I guess so,'' said Grace fiddling with her hair.

''Right, so how about tomorrow night 6pm?'' asked
Lucy.

''Ok works for me,'' said Katy.

''Yep works for me to,'' replied Grace.

''I'll see what I can find out,'' said Lucy.

Three hours later, Lucy's friends had all gone home and
the Lees were sat around their small wooden dining
table eating Chinese takeaway. You know the ones in
the little boxes with a side of prawn crackers. Lucy had
it nearly every night. The Lees were all sat around the
table in silence picking at their noodles. Nobody really
talked at the dinner table.

''Err so what's the lab like?'' asked Lucy.

''Err well,'' said Mr Lee in-between mouthfuls of
noodles, ''why are you asking?''

''Just wanted to know,'' said Lucy.

Now Lucy didn't really feel like she connected with her
parents. They never really talked to her or asked her
whether she was ok and most importantly they never
said, "I love you". Annoyed by her thoughts, she
pushed her plate away and stomped up the stairs. Her
parents looked up from their plates, ignored her and

turned back to their empty plates. Lucy's parents always looked miserable and for some reason she thought she knew why. Lucy opened her bedroom door, stomped inside her room and slammed the door shut. This startled Mr Lee who was half asleep and his tie was in his coffee. Lucy sat on her bed and soon fell fast asleep.

INSIDE THE LAB!

It was the next day and it was lovely and sunny outside. Lucy had woken up with butterflies in her stomach because today was the day she, Katy and Grace were going to sneak into the Lab. It was 3 o' clock in the morning and Lucy slipped out of bed and into her slippers that were always at the side of her bed. She slipped into her dressing gown and climbed out of bed and into the hallway. She climbed down the stairs and the stairs creaked with her weight. She got to the bottom and peered round the corner and checked to see whether anybody was there. Nobody seemed to be down stairs. She grabbed her phone and face timed her two best friends. They were already dressed in all black and were ready to sneak into the lab.

"Guys we're not going 'till 6pm you know at night," said Lucy.

"I'm guessing you didn't see the text then," said Grace.

Lucy pulled out her phone and read the text message that Katy & Grace had sent her: 'How about we sneak in at six in the morning? Love Katy & Grace.'

"Well ok - you guys come over to my house and……" said Lucy. She paused and listened. There was a quiet knock on the door. "Guys you didn't even give me chance to get dressed," exclaimed Lucy.

"Sorry I was already dressed," said Katy.

"How about you guys get some snacks from the cupboard and stick them…………" FLUSH! The toilet flushed and Grace, Katy and Lucy froze to the spot. If one of Lucy's parents found out about their plan, everything would be ruined.

Luckily Lucy's dad had gone back to bed and was snoring his head off. "Phew!" said Lucy. Katy & Grace went off to go and find some snacks and Lucy quietly climbed up the stairs and snuck into her bedroom. She got into her black leggings, top and jumper. She grabbed her rucksack filled with information but because she couldn't get much. She mainly had spy gear. She rushed down stairs and joined her two best friends.

"We got snacks," said Grace

"Good…you guys ready?" said Lucy

"Let's go," said Grace.

The girls quietly unlocked the door and closed it behind them. They quietly snuck down the street and luckily the lab was wasn't too far away. In 10 minutes time they arrived at the lab, but unfortunately the door would not budge.

"How are we going to get in?" asked Katy.

"Look, there is a number pad!" exclaimed Katy.

"What would the code be?" asked Lucy

"I've got it!" exclaimed Grace. "Your parents taught you that number trick with your nine time's tables. "Yeah," said Lucy.

"And which one did you always struggle with?" asked Grace.

"Six times nine."

"So what if the answer to six times nine is the code?" Grace tapped in the answer and it made a little bloop noise.

"We did it!" exclaimed Grace. "The answer was 54" she said. All three girls pushed open the doors to the lab.

"I'm so excited!" said Katy. "I know!" said Lucy.

Inside the lab, it was dark and desolate. The moon was shining down on the girls through the window. Lucy wondered around until she found a light switch. She flicked it on and, as she did so, the lab came to life. All three girls looked around the lab in amazement. How come their parents didn't tell them about this place? Now let's take a break from the story. You see Grace and Katy's parents were always honest with them and always made sure they were safe, but Grace and Katy's parents had something in common with the Lees. Whenever Grace or Katy asked about the lab, they went all quiet and it was always very awkward.

Back to the story. Lucy turned round as quick as lightening as she heard a rustle.
"What?! I am hungry!" said Katy as she pulled out a bag of cheese and onion crisps.

"Katy you could have picked up a bag of crisps that don't REEK!" said Lucy.

"Well they are my favourite flavour of crisps," said Katy as she tried to open the packet.

"Guys we can't get into an argum……………"

BANG! "I got the crisps open."
"And all over the floor KATY!" said Grace
"Sorry," said Katy as she screwed up her face and carried on eating her crisps.

When the girls finished cleaning up the mess, Katy had made, they wondered around the lab for anything interesting to look at.

"Hey guys I got to thinking, if they have a security lock

on the door wouldn't there be security cameras?" said Grace.

"She does have a point," said Lucy

Meanwhile, over in a far corner, Katy found a dusty, old chalkboard with pictures and diagrams. Katy looked at the old chalkboard in amazement and then her face dropped. She had seen a picture of a world and it had plumes of smoke coming off it. Then she looked at the next picture. It was even worse. It was a picture of the world exploding. Katy let out a little yelp and Grace and Lucy came rushing over and they too were horrified by the things they saw. For a minute everything was silent.

"WHAT IS THAT!?" whispered Lucy.

"The earth…….. well I think," replied Grace.

"Well I guess we found what we were looking for," said Katy and with that she pulled out her phone and took a picture of the chalkboard.

"Well I best be going," said Lucy

"Yeah me too," said Grace.

"Same with me," sighed Katy. "Do you guys know what that picture meant?" she asked looking back at the chalkboard.

"No idea," said Grace.

"Well I am going to find out," said Katy triumphantly!

WHAT THE CHALKBOARD MEANT!

Katy sat in her room the next day. She was determined to find out what the chalkboard meant. Her parents were baffled by the picture she showed them. They asked her where she had got it from. She said she had found it on the internet, but by now you probably know that she was lying. Katy had searched slate.com; heavens above.com; space.com; sky and telescope.com and loads more but none of them explained that picture. Katy was about to give up when she had a look on one last website. "That's it," she said as she jumped off her bed. She vigorously typed in NASA wondering why she hadn't done before. The exact same picture she saw on the chalkboard appeared and it had a definition underneath. She read it and wished she could go back in time. She got out her phone and called Grace and Lucy.

"Guys I found out what that picture meant," said Katy.
"Well tell us," said Lucy.
Katy read out the definition. There was a long pause before anyone spoke.
"Wait! So the earth is dying because of cars and pollution and plastic?" said Lucy through her tears.

"I guess so," said Katy. "Should we tell our parents?"
"No way! That would get us in more trouble and our parents probably already know," said Grace.

"She has a point," said Lucy.
"I guess so," said Katy with a sigh.
"But wait, what about the definition?" said Grace.
"What about it?" said Katy.

"We need to do something about our planet dying. It is terrible!" said Grace.
"Well how about we investigate at your house?" suggested Lucy.
"I guess so," said Grace.

It was the next day and all three girls were down stairs in Grace's living room. They were flicking through different books that Grace's Mum had brought home from the lab.
"This is boring," moaned Katy.
"No it's not," said Grace.
"Why don't we put on the news?" suggested Grace.
"Fine!" said Katy
Grace switched on the TV and there was breaking news. It was about climate change. The reporter said there was a climate change strike on Saturday 13 of November and people were going to protest against climate change and pollution. As soon as Grace heard this, she shot up out of her chair and ran into the kitchen. She came back holding a pen and pad.
"What are you doing? asked Lucy.
"Preparing a speech for the protest, what do you think?" said Grace.
"You aren't going to that protest, are you?" questioned Katy.
"Of course I am," said Grace.
She started scribbling down ideas. To Katy and Lucy it seemed like every two minutes Grace ripped off a piece of paper from the pad and threw it into the bin.

"Done!" said Grace, carefully taking the finished speech and folding it into her pocket.

"Are you guys going to the protest with me?" asked Grace.

"Well its Saturday the 13th and I don't have any plans," said Lucy

"Neither do I," said Katy.

"So that's settled then we're going to the protest tomorrow," said Grace squealing!

THE PROTEST!

It was the day of the protest and Grace, Katy and Lucy were in the car on their way to town.

"I am so excited!" said Grace.

"Where are we now?" said Katy bored looking out of the window.

"We're here," said Grace's Dad. "You girls got all your signs and speech?" he asked.

"Yep," said Grace jumping out of the car shortly followed by Lucy and Katy.

"Right come on then," said Katy.

After a couple of minutes, they arrived in the town centre where there was a stage and a group of people.

"Look, there is a good spot," said Grace pointing at an empty space.

The girls ran over and waited for something to happen.

"What are we supposed to do?" asked Grace.

But Grace's train of thought was interrupted by a loud

voice on a speaker calling her name!

"Go on Grace," said Lucy ushering her up to the front of the stage.

"You may start," said the loud voice on the speaker. There was silence until Lucy, Katy and Grace's Dads started clapping. Then Grace started her speech.

"Hello, my name is Grace. I am here today to talk about climate change. It is a big issue that has not been dealt with enough. However, I want to change that. Climate change is the process of our planet warming up. The earth has warmed by an average of 1 degrees in the last century and although that doesn't sound like much, it means big things for people and wildlife around the globe. Unfortunately, rising temperatures don't just mean that we will get nice weather. The changing climate will actually make our weather more extreme and unpredictable. As temperatures rise, some areas will get wetter and lots of animals and humans could find they're not able to adapt to their changing climate."

As Grace looked up, she saw people nodding and cheering. She was filled with joy!

"Animals are dying because of the things we put into the ocean...and as a matter of fact we are breathing in a packet of cigarettes a day so please help me to save our planet. Thank you!"

"WHOOO!" As Grace looked around people cheered and clapped. She stepped down from the stage and was greeted by Lucy and Katy.

"That was AMAZING!" said Grace.

"I am so proud of you," said Grace's dad hugging her.

"Thanks dad," said Grace hugging her Dad back.

"Let's go to Ben and Jerry's and get an ice cream, hey," suggested Grace's Dad.

"Sure!" said Grace.

They all walked off feeling happy and that was the end of that.

30 YEARS FROM NOW

It was 2039 and Lucy and Katy where at home chilling. They had now moved on from their lives as ten year olds. Lucy had a job as an actor in Hollywood. Katy had a job in America as an artist. Grace's speech all those years ago had paid off. A couple of days after there was a knock on Grace's door. She was told that her speech was so moving that she had inspired loads of people. She got really interested in politics and climate change and she is now a politician and an activist.

Santa Chronicles

Rose Ford

Y6

I want to tell you a true story of Santa from a girl's point of view and she was called Benjamina and yes this is a Christmas tale. When you start reading this chronicle you will definitely not want to put it down.

 It was Christmas Eve and Benjamina (she was 8) couldn't get to sleep, neither could her big brother Larry, (he was 14) Benjamina was too excited to sleep. She kept her eyes wide open making squealing noises which kept Larry up. In the middle of the night they both heard a noise like an asteroid hitting the roof that shocked them but didn't wake their parents up.

Larry came rushing into Benjamin's room. "What in the world was that?!" Larry shouted   "shhh you're gonna wake Mummy and Daddy up and also I think Santa is on the roof," whispered Benjamina. Larry said," yes of course that was Santa. He's definitely real, why don't you go up there and see him?" Benjamina said, "Ok then I always wanted to see Santa".

"No that was sarcasm (looks around and notices she has already gone out the window) oh she's already gone out the window" moaned Larry.

Larry went out of the window trying to get Benjamina down from the roof realising he had a fear of heights and was now screaming at the top of his voice! Larry stopped screaming because his sister hit him as hard as she could for being a cry baby. Larry followed Benjamina because he knew the smack would get worse if he didn't stop squealing.

When they went round the roof to the chimney, Benjamina saw something, but nearly slipped off the side of the roof. Larry luckily caught Benjamina. If it wasn't for him, she would be in hospital. Then, when she got back on the roof, she knew she did see something, but she wasn't sure what she saw.

Benjamina knew what she saw, it was Santa but she could only see the bottom half of him because the top half of him was in the chimney. They heard a noise it was the noise of what she thought was a depressed strangled bird but then she realised that it was Santa begging for help.

They said, "is that you Santa?" He said, "yes" but in a sad way. Santa was obviously too big to go down their narrow chimney so the best way to get him out was by pulling him out with the reindeers help. Benjamina and Larry saw a sleigh parked on the side of the house so they attached Santa to the sleigh and told the reindeer to pull him out by riding as fast as they could.

After they got Santa out he said, "please can you help me deliver presents to all the houses?" "Yes please," they both said. They delivered presents to all the houses and then went back home and went to bed. They got woken up with a worldwide scream……

I know what happened in this story because I was there, and everywhere. In the end, a civil war broke out for 5 years because no-one got the right presents on Christmas Day.

Necessary Dreams

Katie Kean

Year 6

One night, when I was 5, my Grandad read me a book (which, in my opinion, was pretty boring) whilst I was in bed. But half way through it, he fell asleep and I started laughing really hard because his head fell back so far and so fast that it looked really funny (like his head was on backwards!) And, because my snorting blurted out of my mouth so suddenly, he woke back up again. With this, I laughed harder than ever!

"Let's not read this book it's boring me to death" he said as I half chuckled, half agreed under my breath. So, he began to tell me this wonderful story about a really old man who lived getting younger and younger throughout his whole life and when he was finally zero, he turned into stone.

When he was finished with the story, he gave me a really tight hug. Then, he put his hands on my shoulders and whispered: "When you're older I want you to remember me. Remember me as a fun grandad who loved you more than the whole world.......... Now get to sleep sweetie and dream necessary dreams". Then, he strode out of my room and into his.

'Necessary dreams? What did that mean?', but I was too exhausted to think so in only a couple of seconds I fell fast asleep. My dream was bad; my grandad was in it. He was walking down the stairs when suddenly he fell. I woke up, scared out of my skin. I was truly shaken. There was a silence in the air and then a quick rush of wind. My nana hurried in, a sad look in her eyes. My nana was usually quite white in the face, but her paleness had been taken to a whole new level. She was wearing her usual green dressing gown which matched her jade coloured eyes. Her nose was pointy, but not in an ugly sort of way, it kind of suited her.

She rushed me out of bed and down the stairs. Then we both jumped in her car as we drove off into the night. We were going to the hospital for some reason. This became clear as my nana was explaining the situation; my grandad was in the hospital. He was apparently walking down the stairs when suddenly he tripped and fell. He had broken his arm! I was so shocked.

At the time, I was living with my grandparents as both my parents had gone away with work for a couple of months. When they were both informed about what had happened, they were nearly as upset as me.

I hated my necessary dreams.

One night, I couldn't sleep. I had started to let my anxiety grow on me like a plant that never stopped growing; it felt horrible. It felt like I wasn't myself anymore, like I was being restrained by this horrible person who wanted to keep me locked inside a prison with walls of depression that absorbed all your happiness and just left you isolated with only your most unhappy memories to accompany you. You see, I was being bullied at that time and trust me it was not fun. The names the girl called me didn't just bring tears to my eyes; they gave me a bad opinion of school. And I pretended I was ill just to get away from her.

The day I came back to school from being 'ill' was probably the worst of all. People greeted me in the worst way possible. I tried to stay away from the bully, but somehow she still got to me. She got to me so bad we ended up in a really bad argument.

That's what had happened that day and that's the

reason I couldn't sleep. I was petrified that night. I had gotten used to my necessary dreams by then and luckily learned to control them. Though I didn't want to use it in a good way then, I wanted to dream about her being as sad as I was.

In the morning, she was at school as happy as ever! To be honest I did feel a little guilty then. It mustn't have worked because I forced myself to dream that and I shouldn't have done that. But I learnt from my mistake.

This all happened when I was 11. Then I let my anxiety take over me and I became a different person. But when I finally went to high school, I felt like myself again. I found this amazing friend called Rose. She was the best friend in the entire world and was always prepared to stand up for me. She stood beside me like a sister and I loved that about her. I liked my necessary dreams.

One night, I was worrying about relationships; my BFF already had a boyfriend called Harry. I knew a few boys liked me, but they weren't my type: I liked smart, funny and protective people. People like Jacob definitely weren't my type. So, I thought about what I could do and without warning, I fell asleep. I dreamed about a boy who was smart, funny and really protective who liked me. And guess what happened the next day?

Yes, I met a boy who was smart, funny and really protective! He was making me laugh at break so hard I almost choked! Then I plucked up the courage to actually ask him out and this was his response: "You have only just seen me.........I've seen you though. N...not that I w...watch you or anything...ok....umm...... YES!"

This all happened when I was 16. The boy was called Jordon Lims and he was, and still is soooooooo sweet. I married him when I was 21.

And now, at the age of 61 I still remember my grandad. I remember him as a fun grandad who loved me more than the entire world.

I love my necessary dreams!

Exper and Bombson

Joe Mullineux

Year 6

One day, two boys, Joe and Jake were sent on a mission that would send them deep into the depths of the undergrowth.

The boys were sent on the mission to defeat the world's biggest menace, the creature known as Bombson, this is how the mission went.....

It was a sunny day at Creature Ville Headquarters. As normal, all the employees were scanning the earth for threats when, BANG!!!

The building shook. Colonel Exper knew immediately what had happened "Bombson has escaped!" he exclaimed.

Colonel Exper grabbed his phone and called his two best agents, Joe and Jake. They arrived within 15 minutes of his call. The colonel told them to get to Bombson's cell as soon as possible. He told them the cell was at the very bottom of Central Park. The agents ran as fast as they could to the park and took the lift down to find that Bombson was not there! They reported this back to Colonel Exper

That night, Colonel Exper had a dream that Bombson was his brother and he revealed his location to him. That next morning, he told Joe and Jake about his dream.

All three of them went to the precise location. That location was directly under James Brindley Community Primary School!

They took the stairs next to the school. At the bottom, they found Bombson preparing to generate bombs. The agents confronted him. When Bombson saw Colonel Exper he paused, "Brother!" He held out a hand for the three of them. Bombson wasn't exactly human, he was more lizard if anything. He had six arms and a black mask with a skull for his face. He told them why he had escaped and tried to kill so many people. He was Colonel Exper's long lost twin brother who had been turned into half lizard, half human when he was younger by an escaped alien. He said that the energy from killing humans was what kept him alive but he hated having to do it. The agents took him back to New York City and gave him medicine to keep him alive without having to murder people.

That was 20 years ago and Bombson is still a friend to Creature Ville to this day and only uses his powers for good.

The Birthday Nightmare

Imogen Pattison

Year 6

Could you imagine being stuck on a deserted island in the middle of nowhere? Well, for some strange reason I am in that situation; I don't know how, why or even when this happened. All I can remember are the last few days of my life and thinking I was in danger. Was I asleep? Was I awake? Was I even doing anything?! Right now, I am sitting here thinking about how long I will be actually be on this island and will I even survive?

Hopefully, I can find a way to get out of here, survive, and find out how I ended up here.

A few days earlier

One dull, miserable morning, I woke up feeling tired as usual even though it was 10:00am. But even though I was tired and it was miserable outside, I was still really excited because it was my birthday. Waiting down stairs, was nothing! Wondering why there were no presents. My birthday was the only day that I ever got something that I wanted. I didn't even get anything at Christmas! I ran upstairs to ask mum and dad why there was nothing there - maybe they just forgot about my birthday. Reaching the top of the stairs, I got to mum and dad's room. "Can I come in?" no reply....again I said it.... but still no reply. So I just went in!

No one was there so I checked the bed, the wardrobe, the bathroom, underneath the bed and even behind the TV. Where were they? Unfortunately, they hadn't even bought me a phone because apparently "I DIDN'T NEED ONE BECAUSE NOTHING WOULD HAPPEN TO ME!" Trying to use the home phone, nothing happened....but then...... "grrrrrrrrrrr," I dropped the phone in horror. Fear started to take over my body, and then it all went black......

Today

Since that day, I have no memory of what happened in between. It has been two hours on this island and all I have is a notepad, a pen, my watch and a litre of water. "Hello is anyone there?" I exclaimed, but nothing. I looked around because I had nothing else to do. This place was strange. It was not an ordinary place there were things here that I hadn't seen before. Whilst searching around, I found a small area that I could use for shelter. First I found some strong sticks that I could hold very well. I gathered them together so I could place them on top of the base. Finally, after about 30 minutes I finished the sticks. Then I found lots of waterproof leaves, and I scattered them all over the sticks, so the shelter was fully covered (that took a while). FINISHED! I was so surprised that I could actually build something like that. Daylight turned to dusk, which meant the temperature dropped. I had a shelter but I needed to make a fire. I had to find two flint stones. It felt like I was searching for hours, but just like magic two stones appeared in front of me. Picking up the flint, I started to slowly to rub them together. (I was hoping it made a fire)... I it did! What a sense of relief... I amazed myself... maybe I could do this after all.

The sun was setting and it was getting colder, but luckily the fire was keeping me warm. But all I could think about was how hungry I was. I was ravenous! I had not eaten for hours. Before it got fully dark, I searched every tree to see if there was any fruit or vegetables, but all I could find was a small apple on the muddy ground decaying. It was the only thing I could find, so I ate it.

Right now, it is 21:30 and pitch black. I started to get really scared even though I did everything that was necessary but would I even get to sleep? I can't bare it here anymore - I would literally do anything to leave. All I have to do is last 9 to 12 hours (sleeping) then I will hopefully find a way to escape. How was I going to get to sleep whilst it was cold, uncomfortable and eerie?

6:10 a.m.... time went by super slow and I didn't get any sleep. I saw something interesting that wasn't there when I was in my "bed" It was an anonymous letter which lay there on the floor and nothing else. I picked it up and I read the first line, all it said was:

"YOU'RE IN DANGER…. ESCAPE!"

Someone knew I was in danger they had sent me here to keep me safe, but who? Throughout the day, that's all I could think about, who on earth could have sent me here? My parents… nooo it couldn't have been them. What could have been that dangerous that they would send me here to because it was safer!! I didn't know what to think! Suddenly a strange timber boat started to get closer… closer… and closer until it was about to submerge into the debris near the shore. I was scared, no not scared…petrified. Who were these people? How did they know I was here? Could I trust them? A million thoughts were going through my mind.

Minutes later, I tried to get a closer look at the men. They all looked terrifying dressed in all black: a hat, jacket and baggy black jeans. This did not look good for me at all. I had to hide. I found a mini log on the ground that I shuffled myself into but BANG!! The log was light weight so as I got into it, it acted like a seesaw and tipped up making a terrible noise... They heard.... I had to escape before they came up towards me or I could be in trouble. Luckily, I sneaked out without being seen or so I thought. But a creepy man saw me! I ran and ran until I could see no more and I think I lost them, but it was not worth it. My arms began to shake and my legs began to turn to jelly. I started to feel dizzy like everything was spinning then... GONE..... I was back in my bed and it was still my birthday!! Actually it was like the whole day all over again, but better, as I was at home and not on a deserted island.

The Restohaunt

Freya Morris - Lowe

Y6

Standing outside a gloomy restaurant, I squeezed my mother's hand as it was dark outside and I was unable to see where I was going. I was celebrating my

Grandma's 100th birthday which I was totally NOT excited about as I thought it was going to be boring. We walked to the front of the taxi queue as the driver held the door for me and my family.

I slowly walked to the door of this normally charming, quirky restaurant, but tonight, it seemed unusually eerie. My heart dropped when I heard the creaking sound of the door which for some reason looked like the entrance to a catastrophe. However, a friendly man took my worries away by giving us a warm, happy welcome, greeting the taxi driver with a strange grin.

Striding into the ominous lighting of the restaurant, I saw a fantastic scene of people having a lovely time. However, on the other hand, I had a question pleading to be answered - "Why is everybody green?" Could it be the moody lighting coming from a street lamp outside; or something more fearful?

Sitting down comfortably, I had a conversation with my family about how good school was. However I found it boring so I got the menu out and I was ready to order. As the waiter came over to take my order, I really fancied a meaty dish. I excitedly told him what I wanted and he replied with a grin, "lovely choice, lovely choice."

As I waited a long time, for him to come over to me with my dinner, I thought I heard a blood curdling scream coming from the kitchen, but I wasn't so sure.

An eternity later, my food came along with everyone else's. Thrilled and excited, I asked my dad if I could try one of his deliciously juicy ribs. Handing me a rib, I greedily stuffed it in my mouth… However, there was an extremely peculiar taste. Taking it out of my mouth...I saw something very frightening inside it that made me feel a sickening disgust...a finger!

To my horror, I realized that I had eaten a human finger! The foul tasting meat totally grossed me out. Looking down at my dish, I completely freaked out! There are no meatballs in my dinner. Staring back at me are white, shiny, veiny EYEBALLS!

Without thinking, I screamed a scream that I have never heard before. Frightened to the core, I saw the whole restaurant staring at me intimidatingly. Hundreds of menacing eyes were watching me, stalking me, taking no notice of anything else. I slowly switched direction to be face my brother, Noah, staring at me freakishly. I quickly yelled at my mum for help in this horrific situation… however, I noticed that not only Noah, but all the other customers were staring at me creepily, even my mum!

Crying out loud, I begged to God that all this would end and I could go home happily. Not knowing what to do, I noticed a window at the side of my table. I made my mind up to get help. I stood up, ran, and jumped out of the window head first, landing on a car bonnet and hurting my arm. I screamed for help urgently, and slowly turned around to find everyone in the restaurant staring at me from the window I had leapt from.

I especially noticed Noah. He had blank, staring eyes and his hair was stood on end shockingly. He didn't look like my brother anymore. I wanted to run, but I found myself walking backwards to the restaurant and in through the decrepit entrance. My legs seemed to move on their own!! I couldn't help it!!! The last thing I remember was a grin appearing on my face and the waiter welcoming me back to the restohaunt.

Dreams Can Take Over You!

Darcey Greenhalgh

Year 6

Hi, I'm Luna and ever since I was a baby my dad always told me the same thing when he came home from work. "When the world turns it's back on you, turn your back on it!"

But one night, my father didn't come home or pop in to

my room to say good night.

The next morning, I walked into my mum's bedroom, but my dad wasn't there like normal. I was confused. I could see how upset my mum was. I could see it in her eyes. Tears created a river of depression on her face. Questions ran through my head as if there were a race inside of me. Mum said, "daddy's gone!" "What?" I replied confused. My mum said in a sorrowful voice "Dad didn't make it out of a fire in a house he was working in. I'm so sorry my baby girl but he's gone." My face dropped, my body sunk and I slowly walked to my bed.

6 years later

I still hadn't got over the fact that my father had died when I was 3, but I started to go back to school. I was in year 5 at the time. My teacher was called Mr Corbet, he was so kind, loyal and supportive. That night, I went home and sat with my mum for a bit before eating and just going to bed. I slumped in my bed. It was a long day. Out of the blue, a voice that sounded like my father said, "when the world turns it's back on you, be the bigger person!" It gradually began to get louder. I shook rapidly. I fainted and hit my head hard. The next thing I remember was being in hospital and guess who was there…. MY DAD! It was all a dream.

After that we all had a happy and jolly life and I WAS TURNING 10!

The Enchanted Tree

Printed in Great Britain
by Amazon